WELCOME TO
PASSPORT TO READING
A beginning reader's ticket to a brand-new world!

Every book in this program is designed to build read-along and read-alone skills, level by level, through engaging and enriching stories. As the reader turns each page, he or she will become more confident with new vocabulary, sight words, and comprehension.

These PASSPORT TO READING levels will help you choose the perfect book for every reader.

READING TOGETHER
Read short words in simple sentence structures together to begin a reader's journey.

READING OUT LOUD
Encourage developing readers to sound out words in more complex stories with simple vocabulary.

READING INDEPENDENTLY
Newly independent readers gain confidence reading more complex sentences with higher word counts.

READY TO READ MORE
Readers prepare for chapter books with fewer illustrations and longer paragraphs.

This book features sight words from the educator-supported Dolch Sight Words List. This encourages the reader to recognize commonly used vocabulary words, increasing reading speed and fluency.

For more information, please visit pass

Enjoy the jo

D1057387

Little, Brown and Company

Hachette Book Group
1290 Avenue of the Americas, New York, NY 10104
Visit us at lb-kids.com

Little, Brown and Company is a division of Hachette Book Group, Inc.
The Little, Brown name and logo are trademarks of Hachette Book Group, Inc.

The publisher is not responsible for websites (or their content) that are not
owned by the publisher.

First Edition: April 2015

Library of Congress Cataloging-in-Publication Data
Fox, Jennifer, 1976-
Brain food / adapted by Jennifer Fox. — First edition.
pages cm. — (Passport to reading. Level 2)
"Teen Titans go!"
"Based on the episode 'Brain Food' written by John Loy."
Summary: Beast Boy tries to cast a spell to make himself smarter,
but it backfires on the other Teen Titans.
ISBN 978-0-316-33331-3 (trade pbk.)
[1. Superheroes—Fiction.] I. Loy, John. II. Teen Titans go!
(Television program) III. Title.
PZ7.1.F69Br 2015   [E]—dc23   2014040289

10 9 8 7 6 5 4 3 2

CW

Printed in the United States of America

Passport to Reading titles are leveled by independent reviewers applying the
standards developed by Irene Fountas and Gay Su Pinnell in *Matching Books to
Readers: Using Leveled Books in Guided Reading*, Heinemann, 1999.

Adapted by Jennifer Fox

Based on the episode "Brain Food"
written by John Loy

LITTLE, BROWN AND COMPANY
New York   Boston

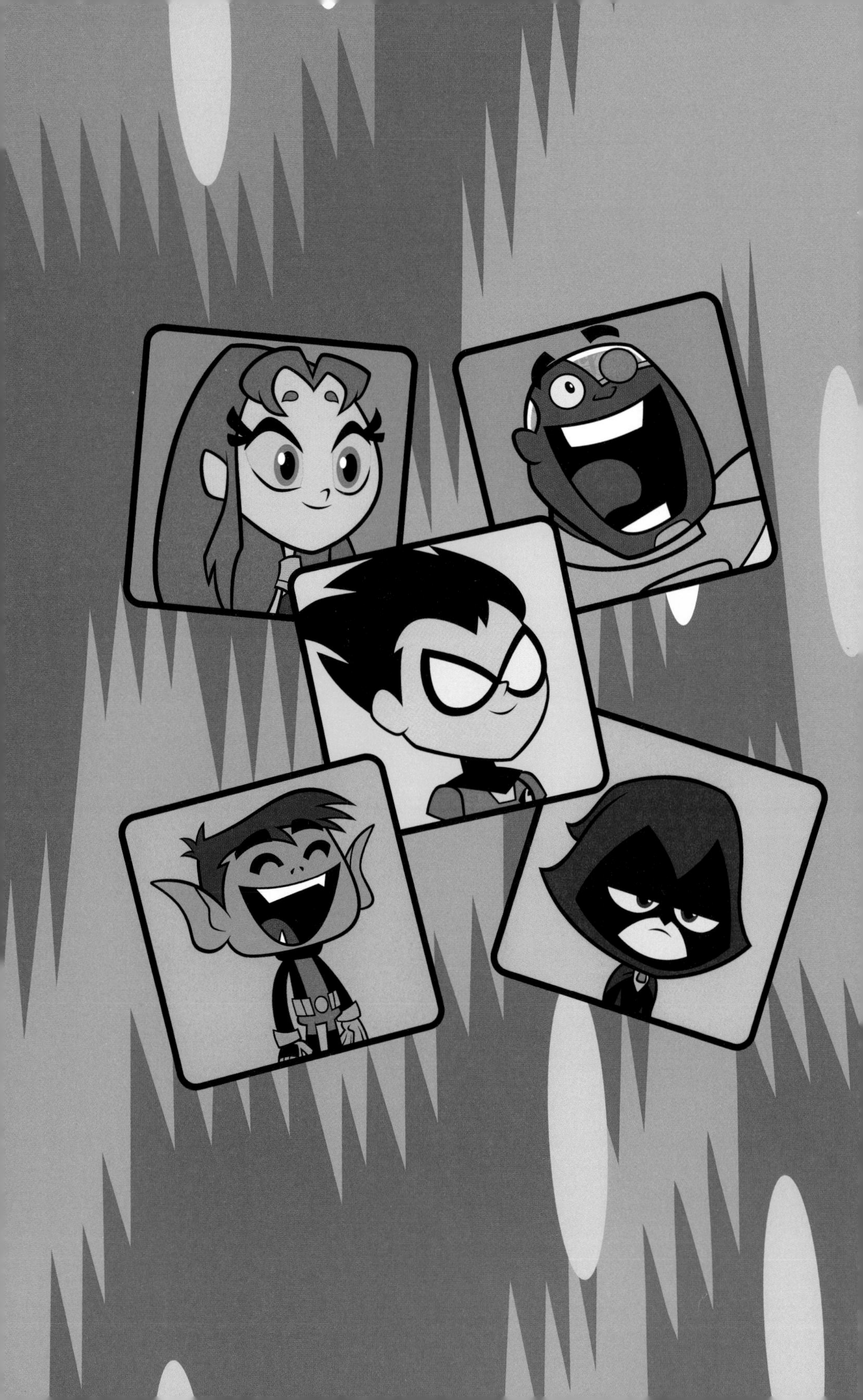

Attention, Teen Titans fans!
Look for these words when you read
this book. Can you spot them all?

asteroid

ocean

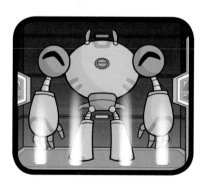

robot

butterfly

"Okay, Titans!" says Robin.
"An asteroid is about to
smash into Earth."

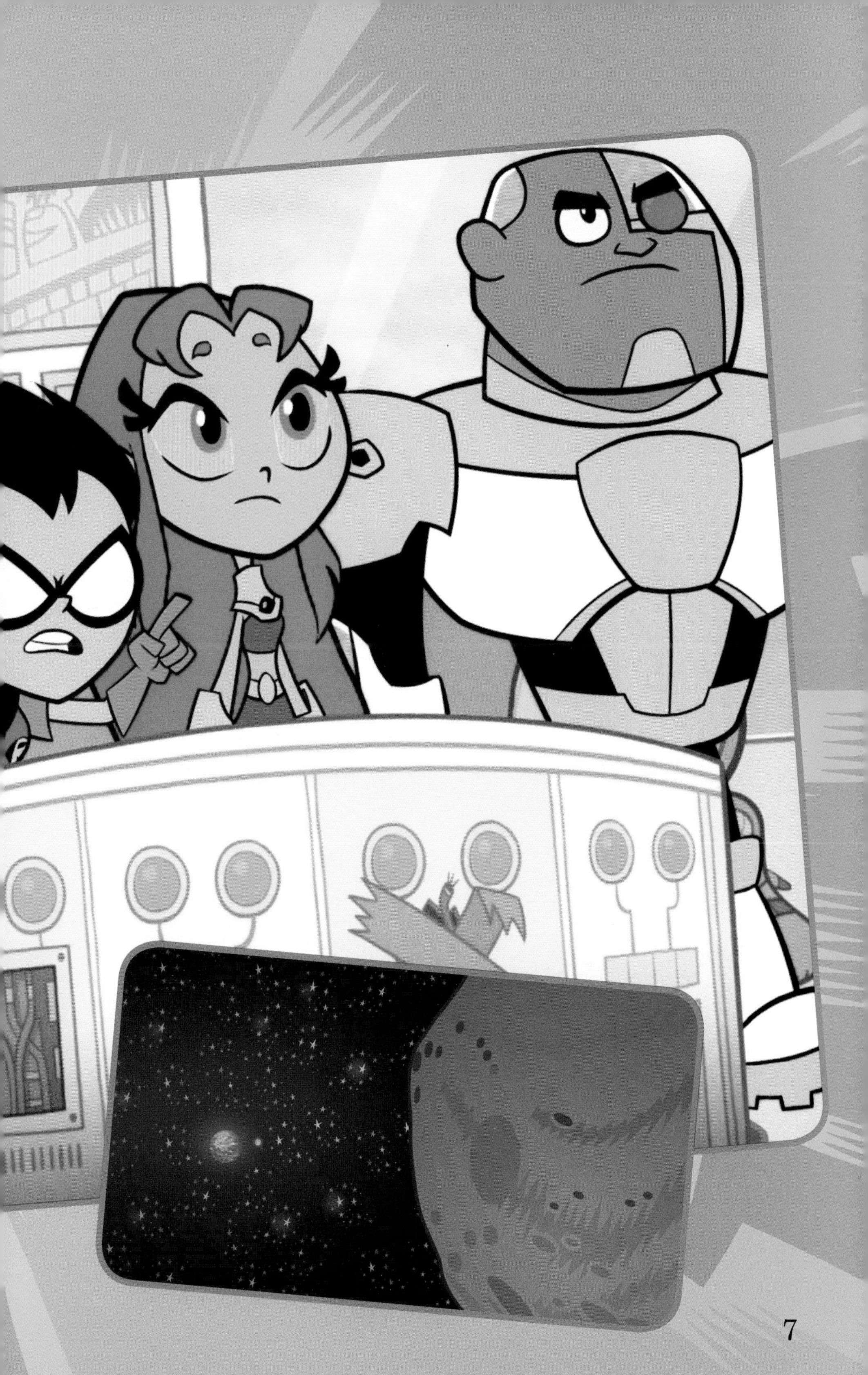

"Raven, see how big it is," says Robin.

"Starfire, find out what it is made of.
Cyborg, build something to blow it up."

"Dude, what about me?"
asks Beast Boy.

"Hold this," says Robin.

"Or give Silkie a bath."

"Why do I never get the big jobs?" asks Beast Boy.

"You do not know how to do a lot of stuff," says Cyborg.

It is true.

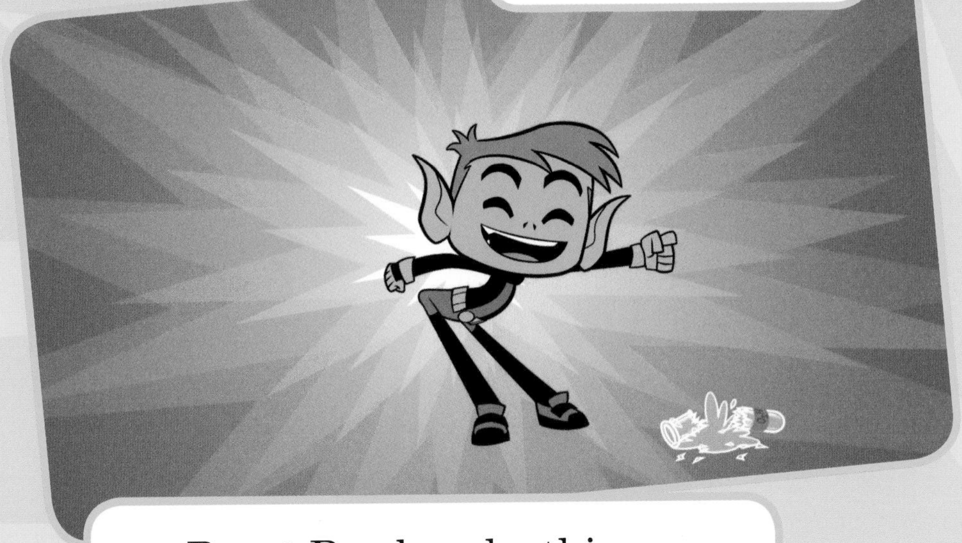

Beast Boy breaks things.

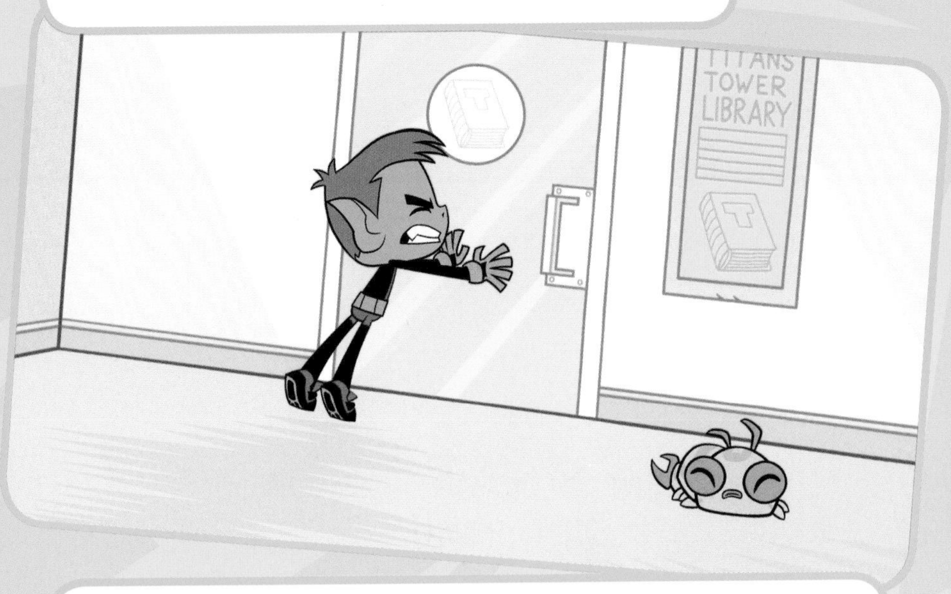
TOWER
LIBRARY

He pushes when he should pull.

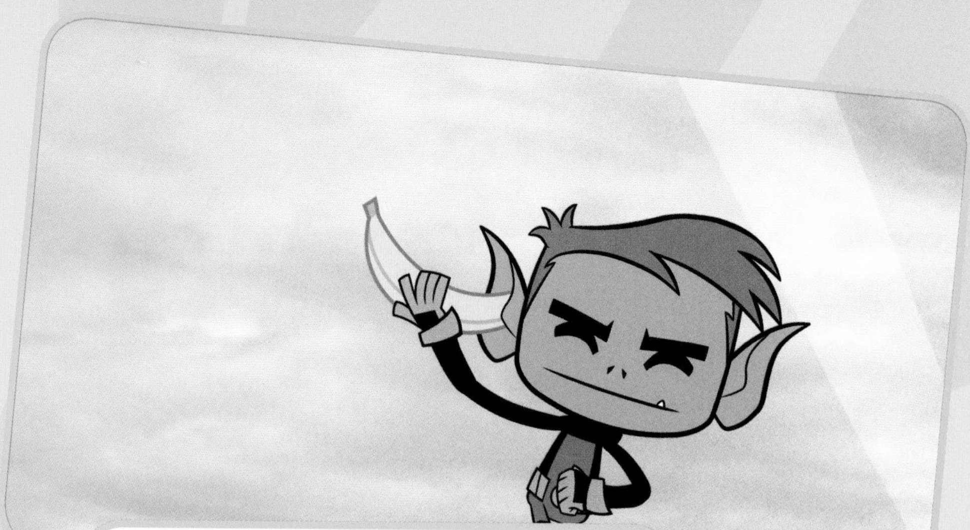

He wants to be smart
like the other Titans.
But he thinks brain food
goes in your ear.

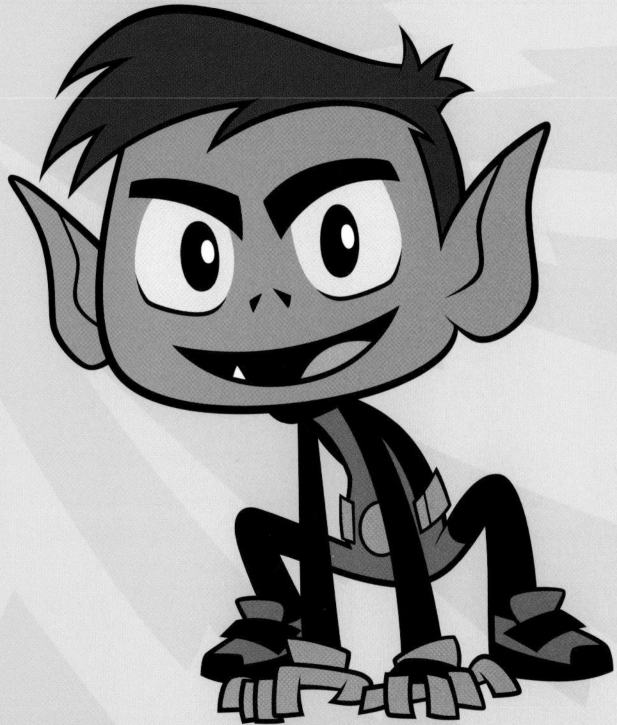

Beast Boy grabs
Raven's spell book.
"I am going to make
myself smarter!" he says.

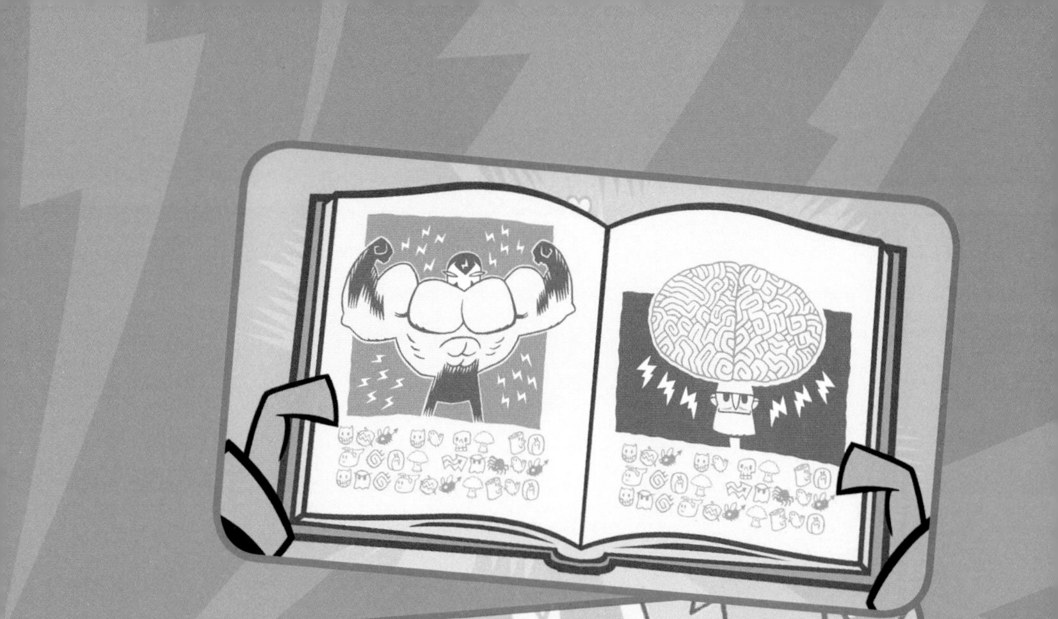

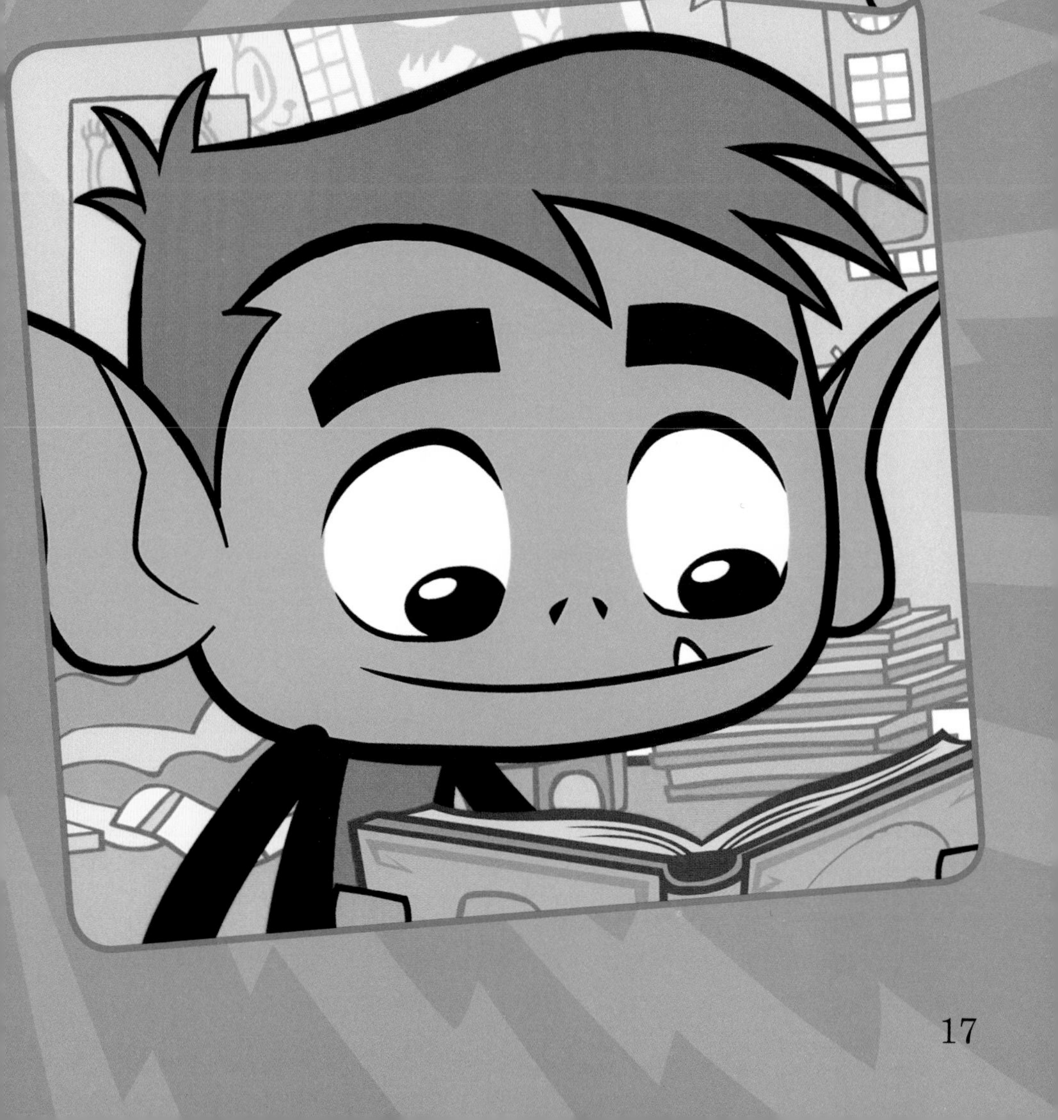

Beast Boy says the magic words.

But something goes wrong.

Beast Boy is not smarter.

So he tries a spell to make the other Titans lose their smarts. It works!

"These bowls do not work!"
says Cyborg.

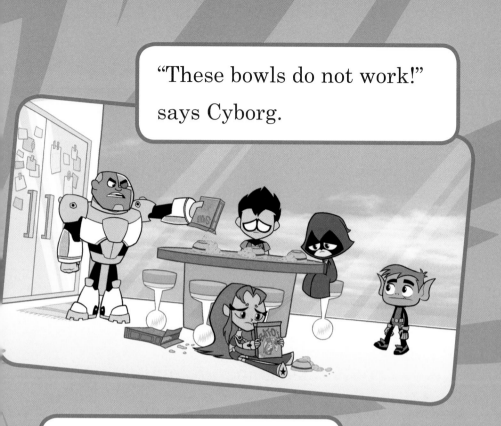

"Hey! Where is my foot?"
asks Robin.

The asteroid is still speeding toward Earth.

"Look!" shouts Robin.
"Beast Boy!
We need you,"
say the other Titans.

Beast Boy thinks fast.

"Gravity is pulling the rock," he says.

"And the ocean controls gravity. So we have to fight the ocean!"

"Titans, go!" Robin shouts.
The Titans attack the ocean.
They clobber currents
and smack shells.

"It is not working, Beast Boy!"

Robin says.

Someone has a better plan.
Silkie builds a robot to blast
the space rock to bits.

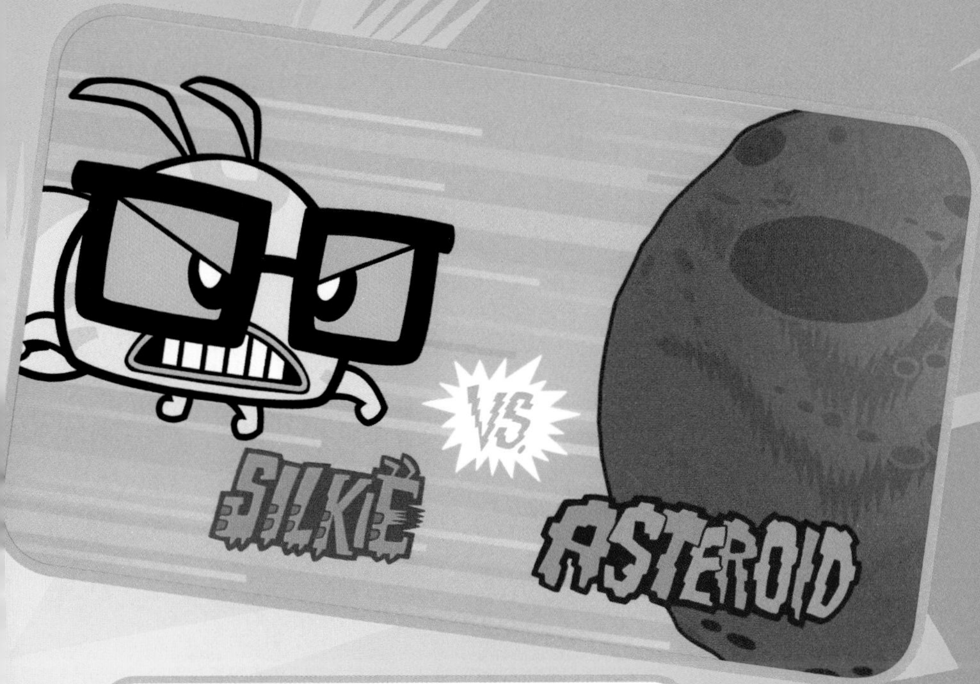
VS.
SILKIE
ASTEROID

The worm saves the day!

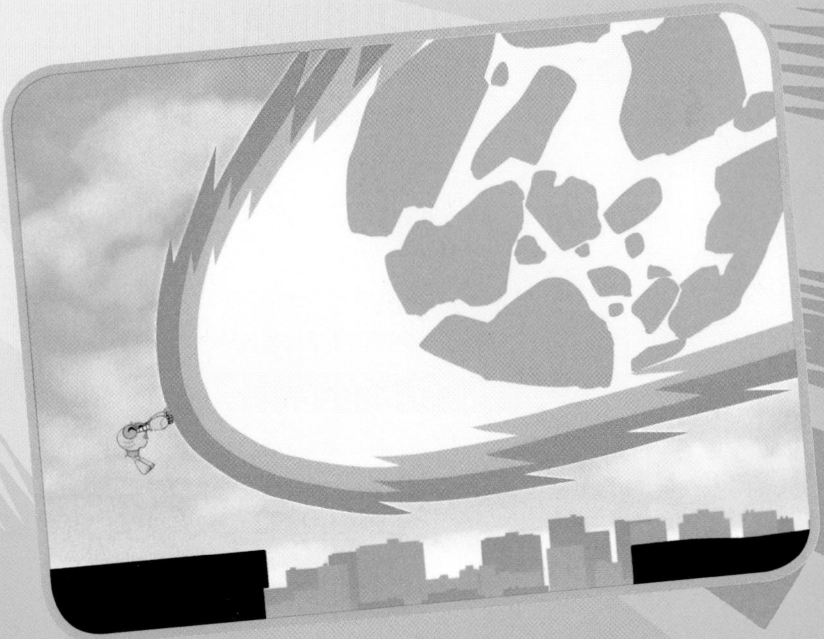

"Look!
The rock went home,"
Cyborg says.

Planet Earth and the not-so-smart Titans are safe...

...until they see a butterfly.
They run into a window.
SPLAT!